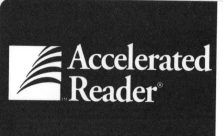

**Accelerated Reader**®

2 0

3 . 8 7 8

Book Number

0.5

Points

P9-BYN-270

# ANANSI THE SPIDER

## a tale from the Ashanti

adapted and
illustrated by
Gerald McDermott

Lakeview Elementary School  15555
Lake Washington School Dist. #414
Kirkland, Washington

Holt, Rinehart and Winston
New York Chicago San Francisco

"ANANSI THE SPIDER is adapted from an animated
film by Gerald McDermott produced by
LANDMARK PRODUCTION INCORPORATED"

Copyright © 1972 by Landmark Production, Incorporated
All rights reserved, including the right to reproduce
this book or portions thereof in any form.
Published simultaneously in Canada by Holt, Rinehart
and Winston of Canada, Limited.
ISBN: 0-03-080234-2 (Trade)
ISBN: 0-03-080236-9 (HLE)
Library of Congress Catalog Card Number: 76-150028
Printed in the United States of America

Published, March, 1972
Second Printing, April, 1973

Ghana

for my
Mother
and
Father

# PROLOGUE

Folklore . . . Mythology . . . A people's legends . . . Traditional stories
. . . as in Africa. Mythology transforms, making the ordinary into the
magical. It brings beauty to the ways of man, giving him dignity and
expressing his joy in life. Folklore prepares man for adult life. It places
him within his culture. With oral traditions, retold through generations,
the social group maintains its continuity, handing down its culture.

This story is from a long-established culture, the Ashanti of West
Africa, in the country of Ghana. Ghana is a green stronghold of dense
rain forests between the ocean and the desert. This home of the
Ashanti people protects their oral traditions. The Ashanti have had a
federation, a highly organized society, for over four hundred years.
Still, today as long ago, the Ashanti are superb artisans. They excel as
makers of fine metal work and as weavers of beautiful silk fabric.
Into this fabric they weave the rich symbols of their art and folklore—
Sun, Moon, Creation, Universe, the Web of the Cosmos, and Anansi,
The Spider.

Anansi is a folk-hero to the Ashanti. This funny fellow is a rogue, a
wise and loveable trickster. He is a shrewd and cunning figure who
triumphs over larger foes. An animal with human qualities, Anansi is a
mischief maker. He tumbles into many troubles. Here is one of his
adventures.

Anansi.
He is "spider"
to the Ashanti people.

In Ashanti land,
people love this story
of Kwaku Anansi.

Time was, Anansi had six sons....

First son
was called
See Trouble.
He had the gift
of seeing trouble
a long way off.

Second son
was
Road Builder.

Thirsty son
was
River Drinker.

Next son
was
Game Skinner.

Another son
was
Stone Thrower.

And last of sons
was Cushion.
He was
very soft.

All were
good sons
of Anansi.

One time Anansi
went a long way
from home.

Far from home.

He got lost.

He fell into trouble.

Back home was son See Trouble
"Father is in danger!" he cried.
He knew it quickly
and he told those other sons.

Road Builder son
said, "Follow me!"

Off he went,
making a road.

They went fast,
those six brothers,
gone to help Anansi.

"Where is
father now?"

"Fish has
swallowed him!"
"Anansi is
inside Fish."

River Drinker
took a big drink.

No more river.

Then Game Skinner
helped father Anansi.
He split open Fish.

More trouble came,
right then.

It was Falcon
took Anansi
up in the Sky.

"Quick now
Stone Thrower!"

The stone hit Falcon.
Anansi fell
through the sky.

Now Cushion ran
to help father.

Very soft,
Anansi came down.

They were very happy
that spider family.

All home again
that night,
Kwaku Anansi found
a thing in the forest.

"What is this?
A great globe of light?"

"O mysterious and beautiful!
I shall give this to my son,"
said Anansi,
"To the son who rescued me!"

"But which son of six . . .
Which deserves the prize?"

"Nyame, can you help me?
O Nyame!" called Anansi.

For Ashanti people,
Nyame is The God of All Things.

Anansi asked this of Nyame—"Please hold the beautiful globe of light until I know which son should have it for his own."

And so they tried
to decide which son
deserved the prize.
They tried,
but they
could not decide.
They argued
all night.

Nyame saw this.

The God of All Things,
He took
the beautiful white light
up into the sky.

He keeps it there
for all to see.
It is still there.
It will always be there.

It is there tonight.

## ABOUT THE AUTHOR

Gerald McDermott was born in Detroit, Michigan, and now lives with his wife, an artist, in the south of France. Though primarily a film-maker, Mr. McDermott is fascinated with the art of book illustration. Of this, his first venture into the book form, Mr. McDermott writes: "Anansi required unique development, to fit his unique qualities. The search for compelling character and design demanded innovation. Throughout, I went to the graphics of the Ashanti people for my direction, to their simple but sophisticated combinations of geometric forms, to their limited color schemes, to their stylized animals and plants." The film version of ANANSI THE SPIDER won the 1970 Blue Ribbon at the American Film Festival; *Wilson Library Bulletin* called it one of "the two most popular children's films produced in 1970."

## ABOUT THE BOOK

ANANSI THE SPIDER artwork is preseparated in four colors. The type is Helvetica. The book is printed by offset.

398.

$15555$

Anansi the spider

# DATE DUE

| APR -2 | | | |
|--------|--|--|--|
| MAY 29 | | | |
| NOV 16 '09 | | | |
| | | | |
| | | | |
| | | | |
| | | | |
| | | | |
| | | | |
| | | | |
| | | | |
| | | | |
| | | | |

Elementary School
Lake Washington School Dist. #414

**Kirkland**, Washington